A long time ago Chris Owen worked on the Red Funnel Ferry service to the Isle of Wight.

When he spent three years in a tent in the middle of Italy, he dreamt of being a pirate.

He didn't dream of being Hairy Mole exactly, but that's how it turned out.

Chris now lives by the sea. He is the author of *Hairy Mole the Pirate*, and has also written a number of sitcoms and books for grown-ups.

Also by Chris Owen:

Hairy Mole the Pirate

Hairy Mole's Adventures on the High Seas

by

Chris Owen

Hairy Mole's Adventures on the High Seas

by Chris Owen
Illustrated by David Mostyn

Published by Ransom Publishing Ltd.
Rose Cottage, Howe Hill, Watlington, Oxon. OX49 5HB
www.ransom.co.uk

ISBN 184167 563 6
978 184167 563 3

First published in 2007

A CIP catalogue record of this book is available from the British Library.

Dedications:

I would like to dedicate this book to Dylan Ford, Jack Seddon, all the little Dennisons, Amelie Furniss, Rose and Arthur Lazarus, Sheldon and Savannah Harrison, Benson Mariner, Chioddi and Shania Smith, and Amy Wood.

Remember you are the future - don't mess it up!

Special thanks to all the good people I met at Camping Girasole in Tuscany, Italy, especially all the pirates.

Final thanks to Nikki Cheal for being lovely and very understanding.

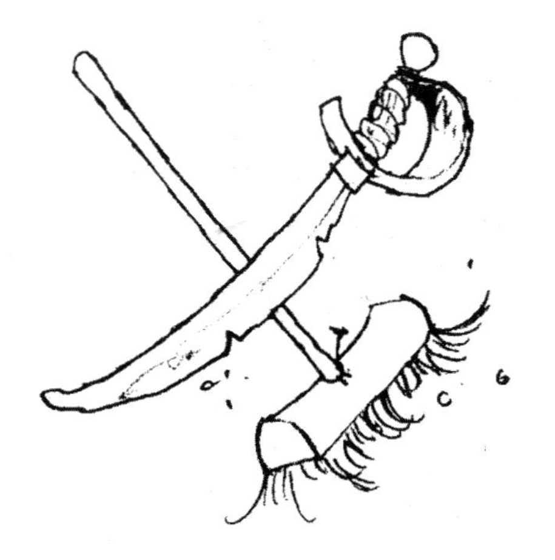

Chris Owen

Chapter One

Contemplation

Hairy Mole sat on the side of the concrete jetty and flared his huge nostrils at the sea.

He could smell the Seven Sizzling SausageS that were being prepared for his breakfast;

he could smell the gentle breeze that contained just a hint of lemon washing powder and more than a suggestion of freshly cut grass from Mr Bernard's wide and varied garden.

But, most of all, do you know what Hairy Mole could smell? Hairy Mole could smell the salt of the sea, he could smell the fishing nets and he could smell the tarpaulin used to cover the little boats as they bobbed up and down, up and down, at the side of the concrete jetty.

As Hairy Mole sniffed and breathed in all the smells of the sea, his mind, once again, turned to adventure. However, there was still the matter of Seven Sizzling SausageS to deal with and Hairy Mole got to his feet and headed for his mother's kitchen.

Mrs Bulbous Mole was content with her life. She had accomplished everything she wanted to do and now she was happy to see the sun in the morning and to watch the stars in the evening.

If it was too cloudy for sun or stars Mrs Bulbous Mole was still happy,

as she knew that they would be out the next day

and this was something to look forward to.

Mrs Mole was also very proud of her son. Hairy knew that he wanted to be a pirate and even though he only had a little ship and a small crew of rag-tag urchins, he followed his heart and tried the best he could.

Bulbous was very proud indeed and she smiled to herself as she turned the Seven Sizzling SausageS over in the pan.

Hairy Mole stood in the kitchen doorway, hands on hips, hairs in nostrils and itch on bottom. After a quick scratch Hairy Mole announced his intentions:

"Mother, I am to set off, once again, to discover new lands,

high adventure,

possible treasure

and definite jam."

"My boy, I am proud! Now come and eat your Seven Sizzling SausageS before they lose their Sizzle."

Mrs Mole busied herself setting the plate on the table while her son continued:

"I have the whiff of the sea in my nostrils and the scent of care-free spirit in my cheeks!" Hairy Mole declared, finally sitting down at the wooden kitchen table.

Bulbous Mole grimaced at the prospect of any kind of scent appearing from between her son's cheeks, but smiled happily at his passion as he tucked into his breakfast.

Chapter Two

A Pirate Hunt

Hairy Mole left his mother's house with a full belly and a shiny new belt.

He had other pirate clothes too, but the belt was

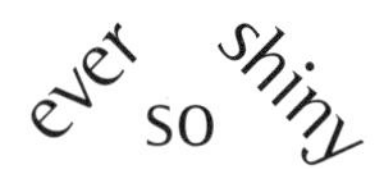

so it deserved a special mention, particularly as his other pirate clothes were looking slightly worn and patchy,

especially around the pit areas.

Hairy Mole planned to sail the very next day, and so needed to gather his crew from whatever pirate activities they were currently involved in.

First he tried the boat yard, as he knew Mr Barnacle often hired pirates to clean the seaweed from his fishing boats.

Sure enough, under a seaweed-covered boat, there appeared a gigantic pair of feet. The toes wiggled and stretched as if they had a mind of their own.

The feet were ever so smelly and Hairy Mole knew that they could only belong to one particular person. Hairy Mole pinched the largest, most disgusting toe and waited for the rest of the body to appear.

"Oi Oi! What's the bother, Mr Barnacle? I be pickin' as quick as I can!"

Pickle the Pirate sat straight upright, squinting in the sunshine to see who was making mischief with one of his ten tooters.

"Hairy Mole, it's you! I'll get my baggage."

With that, Pickle was on his feet and, after a bit of playful wrestling, they arranged to meet by Hairy Mole's little ship at 7am sharp the next morning.

The next members of the crew were found at the Post Office. Crevice and Pit, the twins, were very useful post sorters, what with their eye for detail and their extra-large hands.

The twins were more than happy to abandon the mail for the promise of possible treasure and definite jam.

"Count us in Hairy Mole, 7am tomorrow, sharp!"

Crevice and Pit both shouted together as they threw the post into the air,

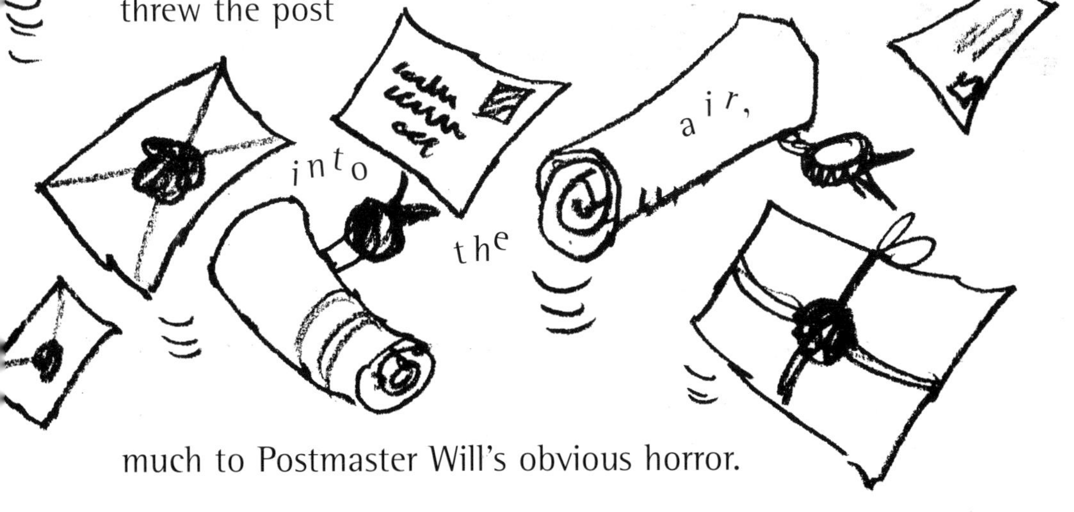

much to Postmaster Will's obvious horror.

Next, to the pub, but not for boozin' mind!

Hairy Mole knew his crew well enough to know where to find them. Belch had spent the last few days in the pub cellar using his giant nose to aid Mr Lockley the Innkeeper.

Mr Lockley had lost all his labels for the beer and had managed *to* muddle up all the *pipes*, so no one knew what was going where.

Belch had been sniffing at the barrels trying to work out what was Ale and what was Pale.

To be honest, Belch looked as though he had been more than sniffing the barrels, as

Hairy Mole

found him

staggering

up

the

cellar stairs.

"I'll get my baggage, hic!" belched Belch, leaving Mr Lockley scratching his head at the empty barrels in the cellar.

"7am sharp tomorrow, count me in.

Woooooooo Hoooooo!"

With that Belch staggered up the cellar steps to get a good kippage.

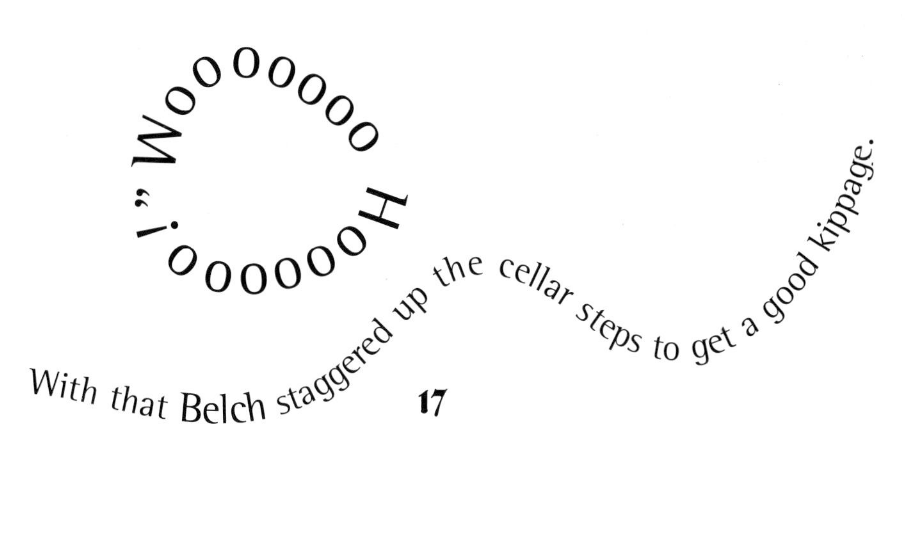

Suddenly, there was an almighty

KABOOOOOOOOOM!

The old cobbled stones under Hairy Mole's feet shuddered and shook.

Green smoke billowed from a door along the street.

The smoke was quickly followed by a coughing and spluttering figure with big ears, burnt hair and covered in green slime.

A second figure appeared through the smoke, shoutin' and hollerin' at the first. Mrs Gumdrop, the sweet shop owner, chased the green figure out on to the cobbled street, hitting her over the head with a cinnamon stick.

"That's the last time you and your ideas work in my shop. Never mix Dib-Dabs with Bon-Bons with Space Dust! Now off with you, urchin!"

With that the coughing figure ran to the waterside and lay on the floor, laughing at the sky.

Hairy Mole approached the chuckling, green urchin.

"7 am sharp tomorrow, Guff my girl," said Hairy Mole, stifling a laugh through his whiskers.

"I'll get my baggage!" trifled Guff.

Hairy Mole smiled to himself. His crew were almost together again.

There was Pickle with his extra-large feet,

Crevice and Pit, the twins, with their extra-large hands,

Belch, with his extra-big nose, and finally

Guff, with her large ears and big ideas.

Hairy Mole continued his walk through the little seaside village, turning corners and following winding passages until he came across the village green.

Stamp, knock. "Four!"

Hairy Mole stood for a while and listened.

Stamp, knock. "Four!"

There it was again, this time followed by a slight spluttering of applause, as if lots of people were clapping with only two fingers on each hand.

Stamp, knock. "Six! Woo hoo!" the voice squeaked in delight.

As Hairy Mole walked across the large village green he saw his old friend and first mate, Mr Bogey. Mr Bogey was standing in the middle of the green thwacking a red cricket ball as far as he could with his left leg. Mr Bogey had actually had his left leg replaced with a cricket bat after an incident in the West Indies, but he doesn't like to squeak - I mean speak - about it.

"Hairy Mole, I'm one hundred not out! This lot aren't a patch on the West Indians!"

squeaked Mr Bogey in his ever so high-pitched voice.

"Well done, Green. "7 am tomorrow sharp" Hairy Mole waved at Mr Bogey.

"I'll get my baggage after tea," squeaked a delighted First Mate Bogey.

Stamp, knock, and thwack. "Woo hoo!" Another Bogey six sailed out of the village green.

So there they were, seven pirates to sail the seven seas with a breakfast of seven sizzling sausages inside the hairiest.

A job well done, thought Hairy Mole, as he returned to his little house to pack his own baggage ready for 7 am sharp the next day.

Chapter Three

Don't Forget Your Baggage!

The very next day, at 7am sharp, Hairy Mole stood on board his little ship. There were two sails and a cabin containing seven hammocks and a table for eating.

There isn't much more to say about the ship, except that it was little and had two sails and a cabin with seven hammocks and a table for eating - but I have said that already and promise I won't say it again!

Hairy Mole stood and watched. He watched the waves gently rocking the ship. He watched the seagulls, one of which looked vaguely familiar. But Hairy Mole mainly watched the gangplank and wondered who would be the first to arrive.

He watched the gangplank and waited and waited.

Stamp,
knock.

Stamp,
knock.

Stamp,
knock.

Guess who was first onto the gangplank at 7:00am sharp?

"Mr Bogey!" called down Hairy Mole. "How are your barnacles?"

"Hairy Mole!" squeaked up Mr Bogey. "How are your cockles?"

Mr Bogey and Hairy Mole gave each other manly pats on the back and stood together watching and waiting.

The next two arrivals waved excitedly with their extremely large hands as they boarded the ship at 7:05am sharpish.

Can you guess who they were?

"Ah, the twins," bellowed Hairy Mole.

"Crevice and Pit, good to see you lads," squeaked Mr Bogey, knocking his cricket bat leg on the floor in delight: knock, knock, knock.

"Who's there?" asked Crevice and Pit together.

"Where can we unload our baggage? Where are we sleeping?" The twins looked at Hairy Mole for an answer.

"Pit,
first bunk on the left. Crevice,
first bunk on the right."

Hairy Mole chuckled to himself as Crevice and Pit raced down
the
stairs to find their sleeping quarters.

Hairy Mole turned his attention back to the gangplank where he continued to wait, occasionally tutting as he glanced at his Pirate's Old-fashioned Pocket Watch.

The next to arrive bounded up the gangplank as quickly as his two giant feet would carry him. According to Hairy Mole's Old-fashioned Pirate's Pocket Watch, the time was 7.10am.

Not very sharpish!

Can you guess who these freakish feet belonged to? A clue – it's what you do to onions at Christmas time (poor things!).

"Pickle, you large-footed mutant, how are you my lad?" Hairy Mole welcomed Pickle onto the ship with more backslapping and friendly time-keeping tutting from Mr Bogey.

"I couldn't tie my laces, it takes so long don't you know!" laughed Pickle.

"Tell me about it some other time. Now, second on the left for you, off you go."

With that Pickle went to join Crevice and Pit down below in the sleeping quarters.

The time ticked by and before long it was 7.20am. Mr Bogey shook his head and glanced at his own Old-fashioned Pirate's Pocket Watch.

"These young 'uns could do with new alarm clocks, wouldn't you say, Hairy Mole?"

"They could do with new bones, Mr Bogey. The ones that they have appear to be too lazy!" grumbled Hairy Mole.

"I heard that!" came a voice from over the other side of the ship.

Now, who could have heard the two pirates from that far away? Only someone with ever such large ears!

"Guuuuuuuufff!" bellowed Hairy Mole.

"What time do you call this?" squeaked Mr Bogey, hands on hips, eyebrows standing to attention.

"I would say 7.20 am, decidedly unsharpish," mumbled Guff.

"I would agree. Now, off you go with your baggage, shipshape and second bunk on the right!" Guff shot straight down the stairs without another mumble.

Hairy Mole began to count on his warty fingers:
"*One*, Hairy Mole,
two, Mr Bogey,
three, Pickle,
four & *five*, Crevice & Pit,
six, a tiny Guff
and *seven*, *seven*, where is . . ."

"Buuuuuuurp!" burped Belch before Hairy Mole had a chance to finish.

"That will be seven pirates altogether then!" nodded Mr Bogey, as Belch made his way up the gangplank, looking slightly green and smelling slightly off.

"I pity your large nose, Belch, I really do!" tutted Hairy Mole.

"Am I third on the left or third on the right?" asked a tired-looking Belch.

"Third on the left, thank you. Now shipshape and ahoy to you," squeaked Mr Bogey.

"Way hey the anchor and up the riggers, me monkeys!" cried Hairy Mole with glee.

With that, the little pirate ship with two sails, seven hammocks and a table for eating left the harbour and started out on its new voyage.

Just as they were almost out of sight of the harbour, a familiar cry was heard from up amongst the clouds. It was Toby the Seagull.

"All together again?" squawked Toby.

"As I live and breath yes, and I have never felt so happy!" answered Hairy Mole, as he stood behind the wooden wheel at the front of the ship.

"Enjoy the moment, Hairy Mole, because sometimes it's better to look forward with happiness rather than when the moment is upon you, and you have no time to notice."

With that, Toby the Seagull flew *high* into the sky and squawked with laughter until he was out of sight and sound.

"That's easy for you to say, Mr Seagull," chuckled Hairy Mole to himself, as he steered the little ship to the horizon and out of sight of land.

Chapter Four

Where Are We Going?

The little ship bobbed on the ocean. Up and down, up and down went the waves. Up and down, up and down went the pirates.

Splosh and splash went the waves, as they splished and sploshed onto the little ship.

"Wooooo!" and "Wheeeey!" cried the pirates as they continued on their journey to the horizon and beyond.

Crevice and Pit worked hard with buckets to splash the sea back to where it had come from. Their extra-large hands made easy work of the job and it wasn't long before the little ship was sailing on calmer waters.

Hairy Mole was at the wheel with a map crumpled in front of him. His big, warty finger was pointing at a place on the map as Mr Bogey joined him.

"Ah-ha! First mate Bogey, there you are!" smiled Hairy Mole.

"Here I am!" squeaked Mr Bogey. "But where are we, Hairy Mole?"

Hairy Mole let out a pirate laugh that he had been practising for several weeks:

"Hoo hoo Haa haa Heeeeee heeee!" laughed Hairy Mole.

"Pardon?" squeaked Mr Bogey.

"Hoo hoo Haa haa Heeeeee heeee!" laughed Hairy Mole again. This time he held his big belly and leant his head back for full pirate laugh effect.

"Hairy Mole?" enquired Mr Bogey, as he wasn't quite sure if his friend was feeling quite himself.

"Come *hither* Mr Bogey, and look at my pirate map."

Hairy Mole held out the map for Mr Bogey to get a proper look.

"We are heading for a country in Europe where the cheese is called formaggio and the fine wine is called bueno vino!" Hairy Mole pointed at the map.

"Do they have eggs?" squeaked Mr Bogey, slightly concerned.

"They have chickens and they call them pollo, so they must have eggs," answered Hairy Mole, slightly concerned that Mr Bogey hadn't been impressed by his grasp of a foreign language.

"Do you want to know the name of this country, *or what*?" grumbled Hairy Mole.

"Well, OK then," squeaked Mr Bogey, slightly concerned at Hairy Mole's lack of thought for his favourite food.

"We are bound for Italy, or Italia as the Italians say. It is to the west of Greece and to the east of Spain and it is in the Mediterranean Sea. The people of Italy are very friendly and sing and dance all day, when they are not sleeping! There are untold beautiful treasures and the *finest* jam." Hairy Mole beamed at his bountiful knowledge of another country.

"I see!" squeaked Mr Bogey. "And are we almost in Italy then?" he asked.

"We will know when we see a flag with the colours green, white and red in 3 **bold** stripes."

Hairy Mole beamed again, thanking his lucky stars that he had found his Young Pirates Edition of World Travel.

"We must be there then!" smiled Mr Bogey.

"Why's that th . . ." Just before Hairy Mole could finish his sentence a loud screech was heard from the crow's nest.

"Ship ahoy,

ship ahoooooooy!"

screamed Guff at the top of her voice.

All the pirates ran to the side of the ship. The little ship started to tip slightly with the weight. But there was nothing to see except sea.

"Noooooooo! Ship ahoy, other side, other side!!" yelled a frustrated Guff.

Sure enough, a beautiful ship with 7 sails, 7 tall and impressive masts and 7 dark and scary cannons came in to view.

Flags of all colours billoWed out into the warm Mediterranean air and the sails blew the ship towards Hairy Mole and his crew.

On top of the highest mast was the Italian flag.

Hairy Mole stood next to Mr Bogey, who stood next to Pickle, who was at the side of Crevice and Pit, as they took their place to the right of Belch, who was shoulder to nose with Guff.

"Do not be alarmed men, these Italians are the friendliest sailors on the sea. They will probably invite us on board their beautiful ship for vino and formaggio!" laughed the Hairy Captain.

On board the magnificent vessel the rival Italian pirate crew eyed Hairy Mole's little ship with a distaste usually reserved for something found on the sole of a shoe.

The Italian pirate captain stood with his hands on his hips. The purple plumage of feathers hung from his hat and f l o w e d down his back as though a peacock had landed upon his head.

The Italian captain, whose name was Garibaldi, like the biscuit but with fewer currants, sat back on his golden throne and was instantly fanned by two golden monkeys.

"Signor Bourbon?" called Captain Garibaldi. He was joined by his first mate, Signor Bourbon. Signor Bourbon also wore a hat with a gigantic green feather, not quite as flamboyant as Captain Garibaldi's but pretty large and colourful all the same.

"Signor Bourbon, what iz thiz little ship I zee before me?"

Garibaldi pointed a golden ringed finger in the general direction of Hairy Mole's little ship.

Signor Bourbon looked a little closer. He had to squint his eyes to get a better lOOk.

"It looks like a little non-Italiano ship. Shall we attack them and steal their treasurez?" asked first mate Bourbon.

"An excellent idea, Signor Bourbon. They will be no match for our 7 cannons and our strong Italiano pirate crew!"

With this Captain Garibaldi turned around and smiled at the fifty strong Italian pirates before him. Feathers and gold glinted in the sunlight as the pirates growled in readiness for attack.

"Men, are you ready for an attack on a non-Italiano ship that looks more like a bath than a boat?" The Italian crew growled even louder to express their willingness for battle.

"Si, si!" some of them shouted, which means "Yes, yes!" in Italian.

"Wait for my command! We will be

c o v e r e d

i n

j e w e l s before the day is done."

"Si, si!" shouted the men.

Captain Garibaldi returned to the front of the mighty vessel and stared at the little bath - I mean boat - before him.

"Do they look like **savages** to you, Bourbon?"

Signor Bourbon had been gazing through his telescope while Captain Garibaldi had been making his speech.

"Zey look more like **sausages** to me Captain. Zee for yourself."

Bourbon handed the telescope to his captain, who placed the lens to his right eye and stared.

In the circle of the lens were 7 of the worst-dressed pirates Captain Garibaldi had ever seen. As he looked closer he could see that, rather than looking fearless and menacing, the men on the little ship appeared to be smiling and waving!

"Mamma mia!" declared Captain Garibaldi.

"Oh yes, they can see us. Keep on waving lads. We will be invited on board for Italian hospitality any second now."

Hairy Mole waved his big warty hand high in the air, as he gave his best cheesy smile to the two Italian pirates who seemed to be wearing exotic birds on their heads.

"Any minute now," smiled Hairy Mole through gritted, cheesy (in every sense of the word) teeth.

Just as it looked like their smiles would pop their cheeks, the pirates saw a small rowing boat being lowered from the side of the Italian ship.

On board the rowing boat were three men. One of the men was wearing a peacock, one of the men was wearing a parrot and the third man looked very gruff but still managed to be covered in jewels and also had a bird on his head, possibly a pigeon. The gruff pirate with the pigeon rowed the Peacock and Parrot Pirates alongside Hairy Mole's ship.

As they came closer it was clear that the Italian pirates were not interested in any kind of invitation of Italian hospitality.

Captain Garibaldi got straight to the point: "Ahoy! You bunch of tatty-clothed, non-Italiano, smelly-looking pirates."

"Ahoy!" called Hairy Mole and his crew, as this was the only word that they actually understood.

Garibaldi continued carefully, standing on the edge of the rowing boat, hands on hips and chest out for full effect.

"We were going to attack you and steal whatever treasures you may aV!" Garibaldi shouted. "It iZ now obvious to myself and Signor Bourbon that you aV NOTHINK! Apart from bad hair and probably very, very smelly bottomZ!"

"What is he saying Hairy Mole?" whispered Mr Bogey.

"I think he is welcoming us to his country and asking if we would like some jam," answered Hairy Mole, his eyes now fixed on Garibaldi's amazing feathered hat.

"Leave this to me, Hairy Mole," said Mr Bogey.

"Si, si!" squeaked Mr Bogey down to the shiny Italian Captain.

They all smiled as the three men on the rowing boat held their bellies with laughter.

"I told you they were a friendly bunch!" beamed Hairy Mole. "Well done, Bogey!" he added.

"You even admit it, you smelly-bottomed, tatty pirates!" shouted up Captain Garibaldi.

"As we are obviously far superior and far better dressed than any of you will ever be, in the history of the world that aZ not yet happened, we will insult you by giving you a box full of our oldest, smelliest clothes, including our pants, as a mark of our lack of respect to all you non-Italiano pirates."

The pirate with the pigeon on his head hauled a box onto his shoulders and proceeded to climb up the side of the ship.

"Quick lads, help him on board."

As the surly yet impeccably dressed pirate clambered on to the deck, the crew gathered round until they all stood in silence, staring at each other.

"You make me want to cry with your smelliness and bad hair! Your Mamas must be monkeys and your Papas must be the frogs!" With that, the Italian pirate with the pigeon on his head placed the box down onto the deck and climbed back down to the rowing boat below.

"Even our pants!" he called up, before joining his Captain.

"What did he say, Hairy Mole? What did he say?" The crew crowded around their Captain, as the rowing boat containing the three Italian pirates rowed away.

"I think they said that they were too busy to see us at the moment, but we should accept this as a gift from their Mamas and Papas!"

Hairy Mole undid the box and revealed the colourful silks and shiny pants inside.

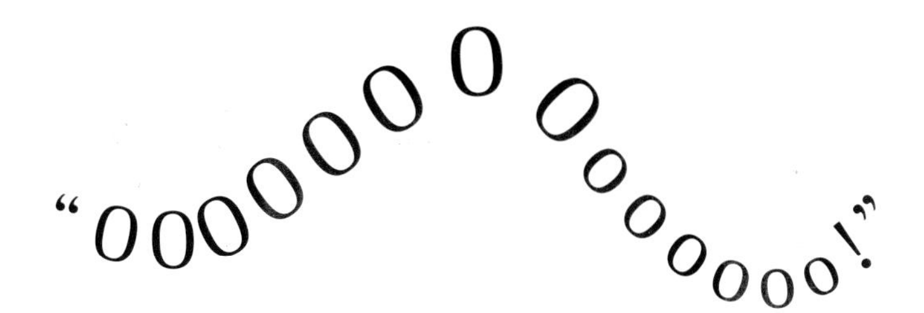

gasped

the crew

as they gawped at the various garments.

"Grazi, grazi! Ciao, ciao!" called out Hairy Mole to the disappearing rowing boat.

"I pity you and I pity my old pants, smelly bottomz!" shouted out Captain Garibaldi, as he waved a jewel-covered hand.

The crew waved back: Hairy Mole wearing a 'new' hat with a golden feather, Mr Bogey wearing a 'new' waistcoat with shiny buttons, Crevice and Pit marvelling at their find of golden buckled boots, and Pickle, Belch and Guff wearing the finest purple silk pants over the tops of their trousers.

The Italian pirate ship began to sail out of sight as Hairy Mole and his crew shook each other by the hands and admired each other's garments.

"If this is a slice of Italy, then bring me the whole pie!" squeaked Mr Bogey. Everyone heartily agreed and they smiled and laughed until finally it was time for bed.

Chapter Five

Hungry Pirates

spiralling

The next morning Hairy Mole was to be found sitting cross-legged at the front of the little ship. As he stared at the

spiralling spiralling

birds in the sky and tweaked the golden feather on his 'new' hat, his mind drifted to his hero Blackbeard the Pirate. Hairy remembered the poster on his bedroom wall with Blackbeard standing with a large toothless grin on his warty face and an equally large, black boot squashing the chest of some decapitated villager, who had obviously been a victim to Blackbeard's villainy and bad pirate ways.

Hairy Mole continued to think of what Blackbeard would do in his situation. As he thought, he plucked at a long curly hair that had started to grow from the tip of his bulging nose.

Poink! went the hair, as it was released from the greasy skin that had been ever such a good breeding ground for spots, pimples and hairs, rather like the one that Hairy Mole now twiZZled in between two fingers as he thought of what to do.

"Aaaaa tissshoooooo!!!!" sneezed Mr Bogey as he sat down beside Hairy Mole.

"This 'new' waistcoat has given me a cold, Hairy Mole!" snuffled Mr Bogey.

"Well, if you will wear it without any undershirt I'm not surprised," said Hairy Mole, shaking his head at the half-naked Bogey.

"I need medicine!" sniffed the First Mate.

"Well, I need food!" Hairy Mole shouted.

Without further ado, he jumped to his feet and called his men to order.

Belch, Pickle, Crevice and Pit, Guff and Mr Bogey stood in line, all wearing their Italian silks and boots.

Hairy Mole began to pace back and forth, back and forth, in front of the smelly, but shiny, pirates. He squinted his eyes and rubbed his chin whilst looking over his shabby crew.

"Now!" Hairy Mole started, and then remembered the look that Blackbeard had on his face in the poster above his bed.

"Now!" he began again, this time grimacing and growling just like Blackbeard.

"I am hungry and I am a pirate. Grrrrrrrrrrrr!" growled Hairy Mole for extra fierce effect.

"Do you know what that makes me?" he continued to growl.

"Grrrrrrrrrrrr!"

Guff raised her hand.

"Grruuff?" Hairy Mole growled.

"Guff!" Guff corrected.

"What?" asked a confused Hairy Mole.

"My name is Guff, that's all. You said Grruuff and my name is Guff!" Guff pointed out to her growling pirate captain.

"I know your name is Guff. Now, what do I become if I am hungry and a pirate?" Hairy Mole was pretty close to losing his patience, as Guff had stood on his last nerve by practically ruining his pirate speech.

"A hungry pirate?" Guff whispered quietly.

"Whaaaat?" Hairy Mole raged.

"Well, if you are a pirate, which you are, and if you are hungry, which you normally are, that makes you a hungry pirate!" Guff proudly arrived at her answer.

There were general nods of agreement and congratulations for the young pirate. So much so, the other pirates lifted her above their heads and started to sing:

"For she's a jolly good Guff, for she's a jolly good Guff, for she's a jolly good Guuuuuuuff, she got an answer right!"

Their song was rudely interrupted before they could launch into the next chorus.

"No, no, no, no, NO!" By now Hairy Mole's last nerve had not only been stood on, but it had been pulled, torn, ripped and tickled.

"No!" he added for good measure.

"A pirate that is hungry can only mean one thing!" Hairy Mole shouted, until his ears smoked and a tiny spot on his neck burst, releasing some green goo onto the back of his collar.

"DANGEROUS!" he bellowed, looking at his crew.

"We are dangerous, bad pirates with fire in our hearts and a growl in our bellies."

"Aaaaa tisssshoooooo!!!!"

sneezed Mr Bogey.

"Buuuurp!" belched Belch.

"Almost, Belch, almost." Hairy Mole wiped his brow.

"I *am* pretty hungry, now you come to mention it," said Belch, rubbing his big belly.

"I haven't brushed my teeth for three weeks!" declared Pickle. "That's pretty dangerous!" Everyone heartily agreed and moved a little further away from smelly breath Pickle.

"How about the kind of dangerous where we attack that village, taking their food and squashing their flowers?"

With that Hairy Mole began to pull on a thin rope that was attached to the top of the mast. When the rope reached the top, a black flag unravelled to reveal a skull and crossed bones.

"Are you with me,
my gang of dangerous pirates?"

Hairy Mole looked at his crew, who currently looked neither dangerous, nor with anything.

"AaaaatisssshoOOOO!" squeaked Mr Bogey in a display of cold and solidarity.

"We're with you, Hairy Mole!" called out Crevice and Pit, who weren't really interested in danger. They were just fed up with fish fingers.

Pickle, Guff and Belch all agreed that it was high time for a bit of danger, and they pulled up their purple pants and began to sharpen their cutlasses, in a show of just how rough and *tough* they intended to be.

All the time the crew were preparing themselves, land - and the little Italian village - was getting ever closer.

Chapter Six

Attack!

Now, it just so happened that the little Italian village that Hairy Mole and his 'dangerous' pirate crew were thinking of attacking was doing a bit of preparing itself. Large wooden tables had been set out and were being covered with various meats, breads and fruits. Huge bottles of vino were lining the entire table and all the Italian villagers were busy laughing and singing while they danced around the feast. As Hairy Mole's little ship pulled ashore, the villagers looked up and sang with glee.

"Guests! LOOk everybody, we have de guests."

Now, as everybody knows, there is nothing more that an Italian loves than a guest for tea. It gives them an opportunity to celebrate how good they are at cooking and how thoroughly hospitable they are to everybody, including pirates.

Hairy Mole and his crew stood aboard the little ship as it calmly floated on the shallow waters of the bay. Each man was armed, or rather teethed, with a cutlass and together they growled like a pack of wild animals (possibly beavers!).

"Almost dare min!" Hairy Mole mumbled through his gritted, cutlass-bearing teeth.

"Wod?" Mr Bogey squeaked back through his equally full mouth.

"I dared, we're almost dare!" replied Hairy Mole.

"Doh, I dee!" nodded Mr Bogey.

The shore became closer and the men prepared to jump on to the sand and attack the unsuspecting villagers.

"Dow, on di count of dee," gritted Hairy Mole.

"Wod?"

This time all of the crew turned to their leader to find out exactly what he was dalking, I mean talking, about.

Removing the cutlass from his mouth, being careful not to cut himself, Hairy Mole spoke again.

"I said, on the count of thr . . . "

"Cor can do dell dat?" announced Belch, rubbing his belly and lifting his nose high into the air.

"Take the cutlass out, Belch my boy!" Hairy Mole advised.

"Dorry, I mean sorry!" said Belch, removing the cutlass not so carefully and just tweaking the corner of his mouth.

"Ouch! I said, can you smell that? Go on, lift your hairy nostrils to the air and get them itching."

With that, everybody flared their nostrils and sniffed at the air.

A smell of tender, succulent roasting meat filled their senses. Fresh herbs and spices travelled up their passages and into their brains; the brains told the bellies and the bellies rumbled with approval.

Hairy Mole and his crew were so overcome by the magnificent smells that filled their minds that they quite simply forgot what they were doing. In a trance they floated from the little ship and onto the beach.

The villagers welcomed them and sat them down at the long table. Hairy Mole took pride of place at the head of the table and smiled with delight as he was presented with dish upon dish of gorgeous food.

dish dish
dish
dish
dish dish

dish

Mr Bogey, who was unable to smell the food due to a rather nasty cold, nudged Hairy Mole in the ribs.

"Eh, Mr Bogey, what is occurring?" Hairy Mole gazed back at Mr Bogey with an extremely contented grin on his face.

"When do we attack, boss? I mean dis is all well and good, dut to be honest I dan't actually smell a dean, danks to dis rotten dold!" sniffed Bogey.

"Take your cutlass out of your mouth when you're eating, Bogey!" Hairy Mole sighed.

"It is out of my mouth!" snOrted Mr Bogey. "The men want to know when to attack. Look at dem. They are getting very restless!" Mr Bogey cast an arm over at the men to indicate their restlessness.

Pickle, Guff, the twins and Belch all looked about as restless as a cat that had just got the cream and then found the keys to the dairy! Their faces were awash with happiness as they communicated their pleasure with grunts, smiles and nods. The Italian villagers were most pleased and patted the men on the shoulders, and the old ladies squeezed their cheeks as if testing the ripeness of peaches.

"Yes, yes, Mr Bogey, I see what you mean. Urrm, give it another few minutes, eh?" Hairy Mole tucked into another plate of pasta that an overjoyed Italian villager had placed in front of him.

"Ziz food makes you into big strong men!" laughed the villager, happy with his guest's obvious enjoyment.

"Si, si!" replied Hairy Mole through a mouthful of spaghetti.

"What did he day, Hairy Mole?" snuffled Mr Bogey.

"I think he said that there was plenty more where that came from. Now tuck in, Bogey."

Mr Bogey folded his arms and watched the men laughing and joking and having a marvellous time. Poor Bogey couldn't taste a thing due to his cold, so he sat and waited for Hairy Mole to give the order to attack.

It wasn't long before buckles were unbuckled and buttons began to pop.

The crew had thoroughly enjoyed themselves and their hosts' wonderful generosity. So much so that they had completely forgotten the reason that they were there in the first place.

As the sun started to set and the villagers cleaned away the plates and empty bowls, everyone sat back in their chairs and sighed with full, contented bellies. Everyone except Mr Bogey. Suddenly he leapt to his feet, cutlass in hand.

"ATTACK!" he cried. "Come on men, come on Hairy Mole. Attack!!!"

"Oh yeah, I forgot about the attacking," said Pickle, wiping his mouth with the back of his sleeve.

"Do we have to?" asked Guff sleepily.

Hairy Mole sat at the head of the table and looked at Mr Bogey waving his cutlass around.

"Mr Bogey, sit down, why don't you? We have been shown the finest hospitality by the friendliest people. There will be no attacking today. In fact, quite the opposite." Hairy Mole stood up with his cutlass in the air.

"Thank you, villagers, for such a marvellous feast. I shall leave my cutlass with you as a gift and a token of our friendship. You can use it for cutting the meat or perhaps as a decorative ornament above your fireplace, it is up to you."

Hairy Mole presented his cutlass to the chief villager.

Mr Bogey looked quite embarrassed as he quickly stood next to Hairy Mole.

"I too leave my cutlass as a gesture of good will. I have had a very bad cold recently and couldn't actually taste a thing. However, it did look very nice. Well done!" squeaked Mr Bogey, a dribble of goo hanging from the end of his nose.

He handed his cutlass to a villager and sheepishly followed the rest of the crew as they waddled their way back to the ship, being slapped on the back and shaking hands with the villagers as they left.

As the crew boarded the boat, the head Italian villager turned to his friend.

"What did ee zay?"

"I think the squeaky one thought the pasta brought tears to his eyes and the hairy one thought the pollo was as dolce as the setting sun!"

With that, they both nodded happily and waved enthusiastically until the pirates had sailed out of sight.

Chapter Seven

Water, Water, Everywhere

Hairy Mole and his six, by now, fat and contented pirates sat on the deck of the little ship as it bobbed up and down, up and down, on the calm waters of the Mediterranean. None of the pirates spoke as they stretched and lazed in the sun.

Pickle dipped his eXtra-large toes into the water, as the shimmer from the sea danced across the waves created by the gentle movement of the ship as it drifted on the water.

Crevice and Pit were splishing and splashing their extra-large fingers behind the little ship, catching the bubbles as they floated off the water.

Belch sniffed in the salty air that made him even sleepier, as he curled his large bottom into a coil of thick oily rope.

Guff was resting in the crow's nest, listening to the far-off cries of the gulls and the gurgling, rushing sound of water slowly working its way through a hole in the bottom of the ship.

Mr Bogey was idly dripping linseed oil onto his leg, I mean bat, as he polished and shined his precious appendage.

In a hammock Hairy Mole rocked and swayed and dreamed of high adventure and carrots.

The carrots d a n c e d around his head, as the effect of far too much cheese for his tea started to turn the carrots to birds, and the birds to leaves, and the leaves into beautiful coloured butterflies that flitted and floated from mountain to wave, from wave to mountain, from mountain to wa . . .

But wait a minute!!! Enough cheesy dream time, what about ... ????

"WATER! There's water!" Guff screamed at the top of her voice, shattering the calm and making Hairy Mole's butterflies disappear into a cloud of fuzzy-eyed smoke.

"Yes, yes Guff, it's called the sea, you clodhopper! I'm surprised you haven't noticed it before!" Hairy Mole raised an eyebrow up to the crow's nest where little Guff was a shriekin' and a hollerin'.

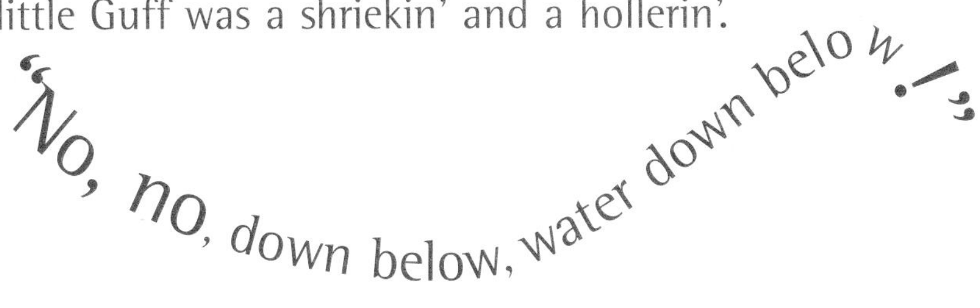

Guff yelled again as she shimmied her way down the rigging.

"Water down below? Well there's no need to make a jig and a shake about it," said Hairy Mole, raising a bushy eyebrow at Guff as she clambered down the rigging and onto the deck.

"I don't know why she can't go over the side like everybody else," mumbled Belch, as he shifted his bottom in the coil of rope.

"No, you nincompoops, we're sinking!" yelled Guff, as she jumped on to the deck.

Now, down in the hold a very small knOthOle from a particularly not very special plank of wood had managed to loosen itself. Now, unfortunately, this not very special plank of wood was at the bottom of the little ship, so now it had become quite special indeed, as the water began to seep into the hold below.

Hairy Mole appeared from down below with a ghostly look on his face. The little knothole letting in the water had now become a gaping, gaWping hole and the little trickle of water had become a spurting, spewing fountain.

"All hands to the pump! Crevice and Pit, get your extra-large hands to work and start bailing!" Hairy Mole's wide eyes told a story of fear. In his head he wondered whether this was the end, was this the way his adventures would finish, before they had even begun? Not if he could help it!

The crew lined up with buckets and they passed them back and forth from the hold to the side of the ship. The water sloshed and splashed over the side as the buckets and the crew worked at a terrific speed. No one had time to think as they passed the buckets that were filled by Crevice and Pit.

The water was, by now, increasing at a horrific rate, and the nails in the wooden floor were pinging and popping as the sea quickly found its way into the hold.

Crevice and Pit emerged like two wet puppies. Their hands were swollen from the constant surge of water against their buckets and their wild, frightened eyes shimmered as they made their way out of the dark hold and into the bright sunshine.

The crew dropped their buckets and looked to Hairy Mole.

"What are we going to do, Hairy Mole?" squeaked Mr Bogey in an even higher voice than usual. Hairy Mole looked at his beaten crew as they stood wet and shivering. The little ship was slowly sinking. Overhead the sun beat down and the seagulls circled, squawking and crying above, as they watched the brave little ship battle against the sea.

"Men, we are sinking!" Hairy Mole began, rather obviously. "We need to head for land as soon as possible. Then we may have to swim for it." As he spoke, Hairy Mole searched the horizon for a hint of mountain or a suggestion of land.

"There, Hairy Mole, there everyone, land ahoy!" Guff yelled at the top of her voice.

Sure enough, in the very far distance, to the East, a small dark lump could be seen against the skyline.

“We’ll never make it!” squeaked Mr Bogey.

“It’s true, Hairy Mole,” continued Crevice and Pit, “we’re taking in more water than we are bailing out. We have half an hour maximum before this ship becomes a submarine and we become fish food!” Mr Bogey was wringing his hands and pacing backwards and forwards.

“We need help men, and we need it fast!” The crew looked at each other for answers, then they looked to the sky.

Something was happening overhead. The sky had turned from blue to white and the sun had become covered by feathered wings, creating a dark shadow across the sea and the little ship.

"The seagulls! It's our friends the seagulls!" Guff raised her hands above her head as the fluttering and flapping became louder. The noise from the wings was eventually so loud that Guff had to cover her extra-large ears for fear of becoming deafened.

A particularly familiar-looking bird perched right on top of Belch's head.

"Hello, Hairy Mole," said Toby the Seagull. Toby's calmness reassured the crew, his wise eyes twinkling as he winked with a comforting smile.

Chapter Eight

Up, Up and Away

Hairy Mole and his crew watched in amazement as Toby squawked instructions to the thousands of circling seagulls. One by one they landed on the ship: some grabbed the sides, some gripped the sails and others clung on to the ropes. There the seagulls watched, each clasping every piece of space available, as they waited for Toby.

"Are you ready to fly, Hairy Mole?" Toby asked with a smile.

"I would rather fly than swim, Mr Seagull!" replied Hairy Mole, safe in the knowledge that help was at hand.

With that Toby flew to the top of the mast and with one seagull word from his seagull beak, the other birds raised their wings above their backs and slowly lowered them to their sides. Again they repeated the process. Up and down went the thousand seagull wings, as if one giant bird was preparing to fly. The crew fell to the floor in wonder and amazement as the movement of the wings blew a warm breeze over their bodies, and slowly they began to move.

The little ship was very heavy due to the weight of the water trapped in the hold, and each seagull stretched and strained in the bright sunlight. As the birds began to spread their wings, so the little ship was lifted further and further out of the sea. The hole in the bottom of the ship began to drain and it wasn't long before the flying became easier as the water poured from the ship and back to the sea below.

"Hairy Mole, this is amazing!" laughed Pickle, as he stretched out his extra-large feet and let them dry in the warm breeze, as the seagulls flapped their beautiful wings.

Everyone stared at the sky above as the clouds and the sun became even closer.

The ship soared into the air, leaving the remaining droplets of water to fall back down, down, down to the sea.

Down below, another vessel with spectacular sails and a fifty-strong pirate crew sailed on the sea. The fifty strong pirates gasped in awe at the miracle above them.

"I don't believe it, the smelly piratZ aV a flying ship. Their bottomZ must be blowing out so much hot gaZ that they are taking off into space!"

Captain Garibaldi looked skywards, and just as he did so a large seagull poo landed right on his shiny, feathered hat.

Signor Bourbon held out his hand: "Hhmmmm! LookZ like it iZ starting to rain!" he mentioned, just before receiving a whack on the back of his head from Captain Garibaldi's freshly coated hat.

Hairy Mole's little ship flew high into the air, over islands and shimmering waves, over fish and the spurting whales, one of which looked very familiar. Clouds passed underneath as the ship sailed through the sky as if it were on a tranquil lake of blue and white.

"Homeward bound, Hairy Mole?" asked Toby, settling on Belch's head.

"Homeward bound, Toby," smiled Hairy Mole, and he settled back into his hammock and let the gentle flapping of wings send him to sleep.

Chapter Nine

A Heroes' Welcome

When Hairy Mole awoke, the ship was slowly being lowered onto dry land. All the locals had come out to welcome them home, and Mr Barnacle rubbed his hands together with glee as he spied the gaping hole in the ship's bottom.

The little ship was gently tipped onto her side as she came to rest on the concrete jetty surrounding the harbour. The seagulls squawked and cawed in delight, as they too had been part of a fantastic adventure.

Postmaster Will, Mrs Gumdrop and Mr Lockley the Innkeeper stood with the other villagers and cheered and applauded as Hairy Mole and his pirate crew let down the gangplank and strode onto the concrete jetty, like heroes.

Mrs Bulbous Mole made her way through the crowd to greet her son and his crew. They all hugged and kissed and praised Toby, whilst backslapping each other.

"My boy, my boy, my smelly, hairy boy!" cried Mrs Mole. "You are indeed a great pirate to return to us with so many stories, hats, full bellies and silky pants. All I ask of you now is one thing!" smiled Mrs Bulbous Mole.

There was a hush over the crowd.

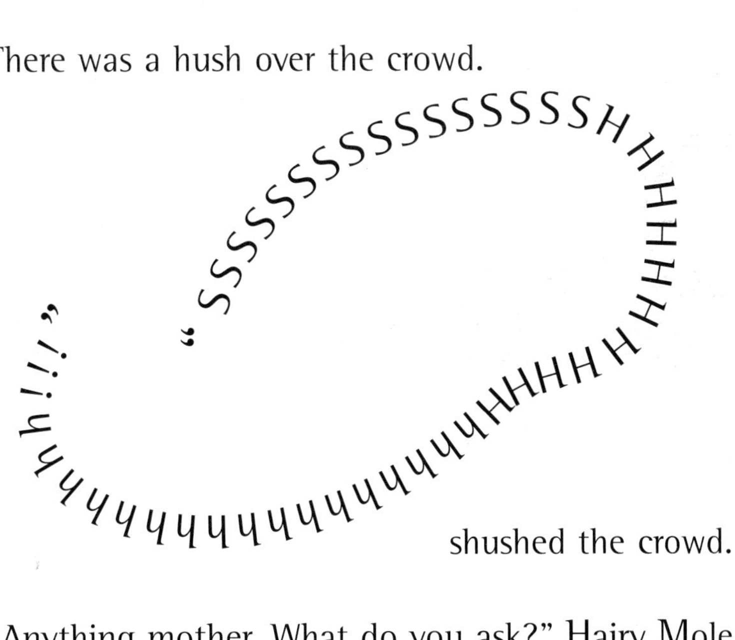

shushed the crowd.

"Anything mother. What do you ask?" Hairy Mole looked at his mother and took off his 'new' hat.

"Just keep my kitchen tidy after you have done your cooking."

With this, Toby flew on to Bulbous Mole's shoulder.

"Fish pie would be delightful, Hairy Mole! Just remember: Barry, Larry and Peter don't like cod, and Helen, Susan and Valerie aren't very fond of pepper!"

With that, a large squawking and cheering took place as all the seagulls flew high into the air and landed on the roof of the Moles' cottage.

Hairy Mole stepped forward.

"Thank you everyone: my friends on the land, my friends on the sea and my friends in the sky. One final thing, as I'm not accustomed to making speeches: last one in the kitchen does the washing up!"

With that, Hairy Mole and his pirate crew ran to the cottage to make a thousand fish pies: three without cod and three without pepper.

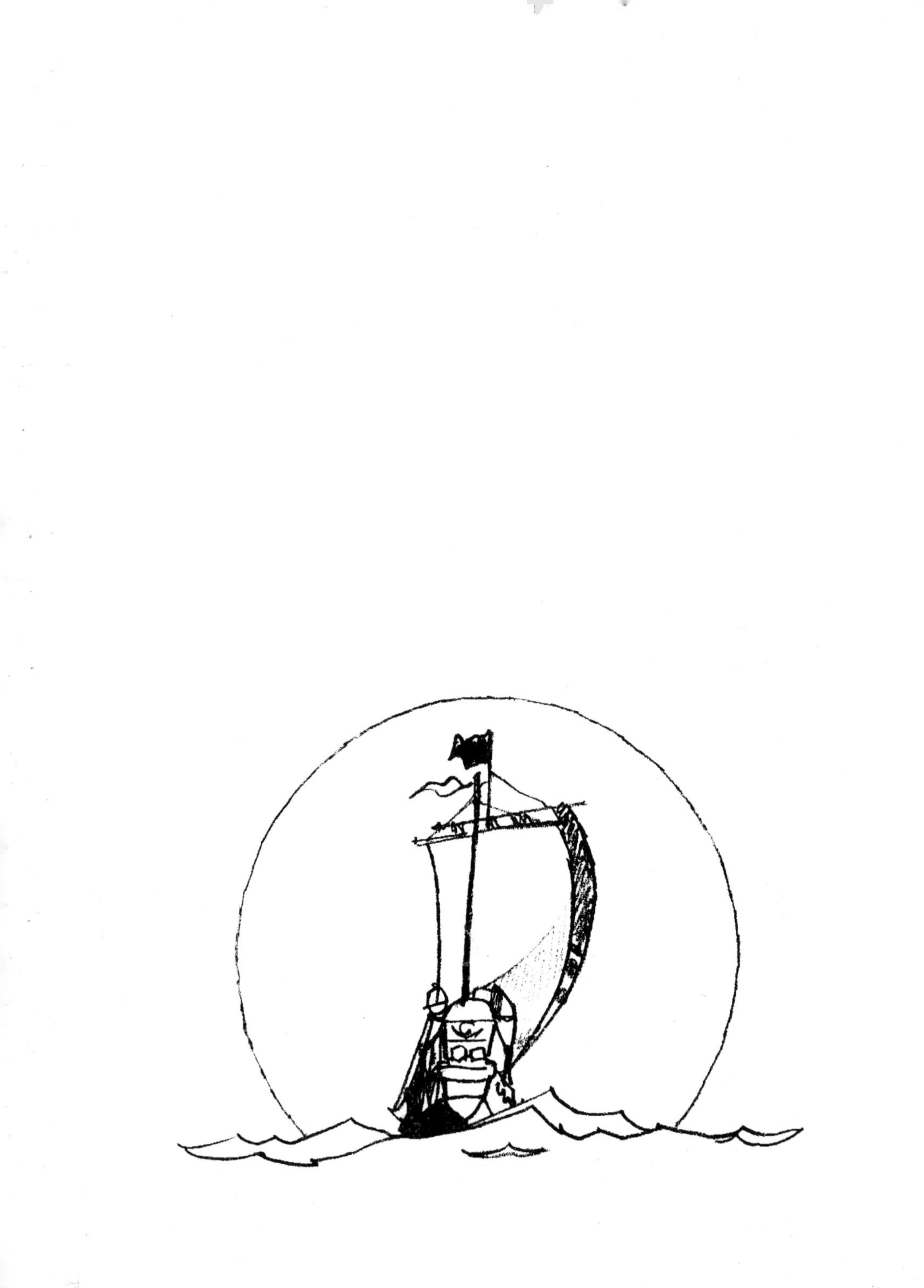